To John Hough

Clarion Books
a Houghton Mifflin Company imprint
215 Park Avenue South, New York, NY 10003
Copyright © 1985 by Donald Carrick
All rights reserved.
For information about permission to reproduce
selections from this book, write to Permissions,
Houghton Mifflin Company, 2 Park Street, Boston, MA 02108
Printed in the USA

Library of Congress Cataloging in Publication Data
Carrick, Donald.
Morgan and the artist.
Summary: An artist paints a tiny man who walks
out of the painting and announces that he is the
painter's inspiration.
1. Children's stories, American.   [I. Artists—
Fiction]   I. Title.
PZ7.C2345Mo   1985   [E]   84-14267
ISBN 0-89919-300-5   PA ISBN 0-395-58176-1

HC BP PA SM 10 9 8 7 6 5 4 3 2

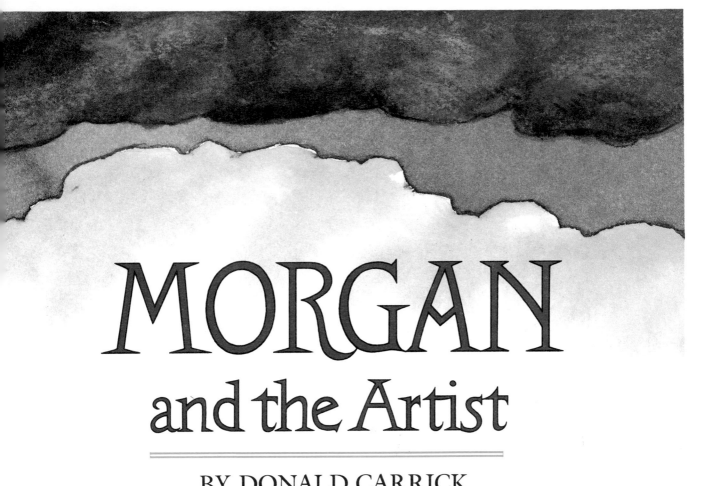

MORGAN
and the Artist

BY DONALD CARRICK

CLARION BOOKS
NEW YORK

As It Was

Frederic Toll was an artist who worked very hard to become a good landscape painter. But he was not satisfied with his work.

Invention

Artists often paint things they feel but cannot explain. One day Frederic found himself painting a familiar small figure in his picture. The tiny man had first appeared as a woodcutter in a landscape. Then he turned up in another picture, standing in a trout stream. Now here he was again. He was holding a horn and he stared straight at Frederic with a mocking grin.

"Back again, Morgan, I see," said the artist, who had grown fond of his creation, even giving him a name.

Morgan seemed to smile. "You look as if you have something to tell me," Frederic mused. "If I had the power, I'd paint a path for you right out of this picture."

Absently, Frederic did just that with a few strokes of his brush. Morgan stirred. Then he walked down the path and jumped to the painter's palette.

"I can't believe my eyes," gasped the painter. "Can this be real?"

"It's real for you," answered Morgan.

"But why?" asked the painter.

"Every artist's studio has a spirit, and I'm the spirit of yours," said Morgan. "You have been searching for your own way to paint what you feel. Perhaps I can help you."

Frederic could not believe his good fortune.

Good Days

Because paint flowed in Morgan's veins, anything Frederic painted was real to him. First off, the artist painted Morgan his own apartment with a balcony and a window. He pinned it to a wall where Morgan would have a good view of the studio.

Since Frederic was a better painter than a cook, Morgan ate like a king, while the artist had to be content with beans.

Together, they visited museums to study the famous paintings. Frederic was amazed to see Morgan jump in and out of the pictures while they talked.

"I can travel wherever there is a painting," Morgan explained.

Morgan almost got lost in one picture of a wind-swept cliff, but the painter plucked him out just in time. When Frederic touched the painting, the guard decided he was dangerous and asked him to leave. Frederic was embarrassed but Morgan just laughed.

"We must find the best way for you to paint," said Morgan. "Load the wagon with painting materials," he directed.

As Morgan played his horn, the friends roamed the countryside, seeking new scenes to paint. Frederic painted in different ways until he found the one most natural to him. With each painting he gathered courage to believe in himself.

Frederic began one day to make a watercolor of a stormy sea. In his eagerness to watch, Morgan climbed to a high place. To get an even better view, he leaned out too far and slipped. Morgan's cries were muffled by the crashing sea. He fell, unnoticed, into the artist's water can.

Morgan soon discovered a new danger. The furiously working artist swirled his brush into the can each time he added more wet color to his picture. It was one thing for Morgan to float around in filthy water, but quite another to be thrashed by a giant mop. To save himself, he clung to the brush the next time it was dipped in.

"Help!" Morgan shouted. His small voice trailed away as he was flicked into the watercolor sea.

Unfortunately, all paintings do not turn out well. Despite the artist's best efforts, his colors were going muddy. The more he painted, the worse the picture got. Morgan scrambled to the edge where he watched in horror as the big hands reached down to tear the picture from the board. With a curse, the artist crushed it into a wad and threw it over the edge to the great rocks below.

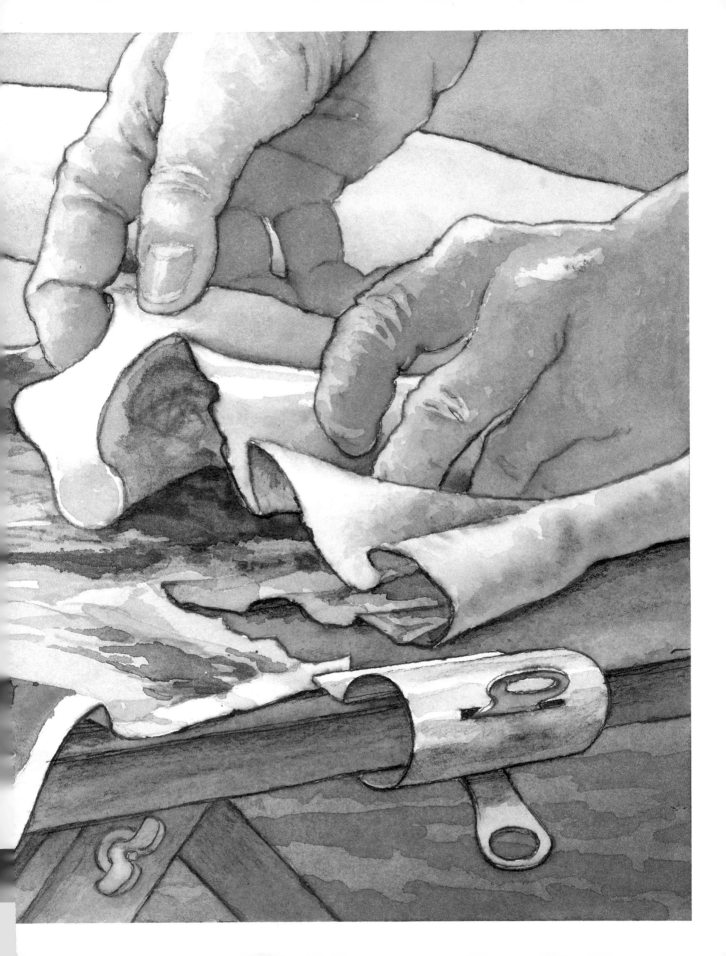

Morgan was spared another dunking when his coat caught on a clip. Spying his small dripping friend, the artist's humor returned. "Morgan! You're bluer than my mood," he said with a chuckle.

Finally, the wagon was filled with paintings. It was time for the travelers to return home. The artist hung the paintings all over the studio so he and Morgan could look at them together for the first time.

"You have found your own way to paint," declared Morgan.

Collectors from museums, managers of banks, and city officials all came to look. They began to buy the pictures. Morgan, who stood unnoticed near the painter, was delighted by his friend's success. He knew the splendid pictures would make the collectors' rooms seem important. Then *they* would feel important, too.

Thus began the golden days. The more Frederic painted, the more people came to admire and buy his pictures. Now he was a famous man.

There was a change in the artist's life. His studio became a gathering place for collectors.

"Your pictures grow better with each visit," said one.

"The best work you have ever done," said another.

Writers praised the painter in newspapers and magazines. This brought even more collectors to fight for his pictures. The painter was very flattered by all this attention. He was afraid to try anything new because he didn't know if people would like it. To be safe, he began to make copies of his successful pictures. This made Morgan angry.

The Quarrel

Next day, the painter noticed smoke coming from a picture on the easel. It was Morgan toasting marsh-mallows.

"Morgan!" cried the artist. "What can you be thinking?"

"Since you are no longer painting original pictures, I took the day off for a picnic," taunted Morgan.

They began arguing. When Morgan could stand it no longer, he dragged out a tube of paint. He squeezed a glob of bright red and ran through it, making tracks all over the half finished picture. "This is what I think of your copies," he shouted.

"Now you've gone too far!" bellowed Frederic. His hand shook with rage as he took a brush and painted over Morgan's red tracks.

Morgan tried to get away, but Frederic was so angry that he painted over the little man as well. Then the artist dashed outside to calm himself.

Discovery

The artist filled his studio with copies, hoping to please the collectors. Too late, he discovered his mistake. The collectors became bored with the same old pictures and left to find painters with new ideas.

Frederic felt as if he had lost his way. The paint on his palette dried hard as stone. Now he was reduced to wandering about his darkened studio, looking for his lost art. He missed Morgan more each day.

One day a gray picture caught his eye. "Perhaps a little green would help," he said, turning the picture this way and that.

He began to scrape away the paint to make a fresh start. "What's this!" he exclaimed as he discovered bright red paint under the gray. As he scraped, the red got brighter, and there, standing next to it, looking faded, was Morgan.

"My dear friend, I've found you again!" exclaimed the artist. "But how awful you look!"

"Of course I look awful," grumbled Morgan. "I'm a reflection of you."

Quickly Frederic squeezed fresh color on his palette and repainted Morgan. "There, my friend," he said. "Now you're back to your old self."

"Indeed," said Morgan. "I've been waiting for you to discover me again, but…" He glanced about the studio filled with copies. "I can see I'm still not needed here."

Morgan stood once again on Frederic's palette. "Goodbye, Frederic," he said. "I'll go now, the way I came. Some other artist may need me."

"Morgan!" shouted Frederic. "Don't leave. You are needed *here*."

"Why?" challenged Morgan. "Do you really want to find your painter's eye again?"

"More than ever," answered the miserable artist. "Please stay and help me."

Hearing Frederic, Morgan softened. "Well...I *will* miss your cooking." His color returned. "Perhaps a good meal could change my mind."

The first smile in weeks spread over Frederic's face. "A bargain, old friend," he cried. "No sooner said than done."

As It Is

The artist sprang to his task. Morgan tacked a note to Frederic's easel. It said,

> TRUST WHAT YOU LIKE,
> NOT WHAT THEY WANT.

Before Morgan had finished his meal, Frederic had cleaned his brushes and prepared his palette. Far into the night the artist painted while Morgan played softly on his horn.